Dear Heart, I trust you!

By: A. Jaye

Synopsis

Soul Tyes has had her heart bent out of shape too many times to count. To Soul, Valentine's day is just another day for a guy to not answer the phone and bring you the discounted flowers on the 15th. The definition of Love isn't to be deeply committed and connected to someone or something. Love means lowering others vibrating energy; that's exactly what it does.

Loving the right one can set your soul on fire, while loving the wrong one, can throw your vibrations off and have negative energy all around you. Making you regret the day you ever felt what was supposed to be LOVE.

Coldon Heart thought being successful was all he needed to do to find love. Forgetting that love also requires you to not only tell but show your other half that you love them. The worst part about showing love is not knowing how. Coming from a family where love meant having money and power, you tend to forget that some women want love that speaks to their soul not just their bank accounts.

That type of love is foreign language to Heart, and he'll soon find out that stepping to a woman like Soul you have to come with all of you, because she can get her own bag.

A woman with her guard up is a woman who's tired of being hurt. Instead of telling her she has "trust issues," become a part of her protection for her heart no matter how much patience it requires. - #ISTILLWANTIT poetry book by Derrick Jaxn

Chapter 1

Soul Tyes

I'm not broken, God's making stained glass!

January 31st, 2021

I damn near knocked over everything on the glass nightstand trying to turn my phone off. My ten and ten thirty p.m. alarm already went off and now my eleven p.m. is about to piss me off even more. I hated being late for work and at the same time, I hated to be woken up out of some good ass sleep.

The one that goes off at eleven thirty, will have a note saying, bitch call in because you're late as fuck. I've been working from home for a few months now due to Covid and tonight was the first night we were allowed back in the building.

I have one of the hottest midnight, Heart & Soul, love letter sessions at Kiss 104.1 FM out of Atlanta. Around Valentine's Day, I get the craziest letters. Majority are from lonely females wanting to know what they are doing wrong and desperate men asking me out on dates. I mean I'm single but I'm not that single to accept an offer like that from a stranger.

Tonight, would be no different, so I wasn't in a rush to speak to the hearts of the lonely. Tuh, including myself sometimes. I mean, I would not call myself lonely because I enjoy mending my heart in peace, but a bitch can get real dick deprived sometimes.

February was the only month on the Calendar that I hated. I

could deal with the hot summer months, the cold winter months, even the rainy April showers that supposed to bring May Flowers, but it's something 'bout that month of love that give me hives.

Rolling out of bed, I dragged myself to my walk-in closet and pulled out a simple sweat suit my best friend Loni bought me. She is the type that would drop off a Louis Vuitton bag to me for Valentine's day just because she knows I ain't getting shit. Loni and I have been friends since I moved to Atlanta from Mississippi six years ago.

At twenty-four years old, fresh out of Mississippi State University with a major in Mass Communications, I was ready to start my new life. What other place to start that then, Atl? My life has been the shit since I moved here. I have adjusted to the extra southern twang they have here, the crazy traffic that I still hate, not to mention the food here is delicious as hell.

I did not even hesitate to start a new life from under my family's wings and far away from my ex-boyfriend Darnell. Darnell was the creator of cheating and lying; nigga did more cheating than lying because he was too smooth to get caught.

Oooh baby but when he did, I was the only person who ended up hurt. My heart was crushed, balled up, raveled, and unraveled again, stepped on and tarnished. Yet, I let him breathe when I should have told my cousins to handle his dog ass.

I flipped the light switch on in my bathroom and watched the lights pop on one by one to the blaring sounds of *I'm every woman*. My mother loved this song and made me love it as a child because I heard it every Saturday morning while we cleaned up the house.

Stripping out of my oversized T-shirt, I tugged at my sheer panties making them drop to the floor. Before my hot water steamed up the mirror that hung behind my bathroom door, I stood there and fell in love with myself. My small petite frame was nothing like the women here, but I loved everything about me.

From my chestnut brown skin to my big curly hair with gold hues of highlights flowing gracefully through the coils.

"Soul Tyes, you are a bad bitch. You are beautiful, you are strong, and you are deserving of all the blessings you are about to receive. You are your own rib because why would you want to be the rib of a man who will only break you. You got this and if no one else has your back just know that-"

"I do!" I heard from the other side of the door making me grab my chest. Grabbing my robe, I swung the door open and started swinging on my co-worker, Heart.

"What did I tell you about coming over without me knowing?" I spat, as I hit him one more time in the chest. Heart ate all my little soft hits like it was popcorn being thrown at him. He and I started working together three years ago. The attraction was real between us, but I would never act on it at all. I could never see myself mixing business with pleasure.

Heart stood a sexy ass six two, broad shoulders, manly thick, not female thick with Godiva chocolate dark skin. If I did not put in my mind and heart that men weren't shit, he would be my ain't shit man.

He had everything a woman would want in a man. Looks, he is smart as hell, he works with me, but he had money long enough to own the company if he wanted to. His smile was an instant panty wetter, and his voice carried this soothing New York accent. It was something about that rude, overconfident demeanor that does something to me.

Lusting is a sin, so I try my best to keep my thoughts to myself but my, oh my, it is hard. Heart and I became close over the years. The more time we spent with each other, the more I started to feel him, but I refused to let him know that.

"I called your phone several times letting you know I was on the way to pick you up. When you did not answer, I thought you overslept so I was coming over to wake you up. Since yo lil ass hate being late." He wrapped his arms around me to pick me off my feet while I held my body stiff as a board. Heart started nudging his nose in the crease of my neck making me laugh.

"Put me down, you stink!" I squealed and wiggled out his arms.

"I couldn't sleep so I went to the gym for a little while until it was time for us to go to work. If I smell too bad for you to sit next to, then I could always join you in the shower."

"Boy!"

"Nah son, you know don't nothing about me scream boy. Correct that," he told me nonchalantly, but his voice still heavy enough to let me know that he was serious.

"Whatever Coldon, that key was for emergencies only," I said as I poked him in the chest and walked back into the bathroom.

"That was an emergency, my Soul," he yelled out, calling me by the name he gave me years ago as the door to the bathroom closed in his face. "My Soul! You hear me?"

Swinging the door back open, I tossed him two towels, "Go take a shower in the other bathroom and hurry up," I fussed.

"If you scared of the D, just say that," Heart mumbled as if I would not hear him.

"A lower-case d never scared me," I replied loud enough for him to hear.

∞ ∞ ∞

"You guys know what time it, it's time for Heart & Soul Love letters." Heart soothing voice sounded like he was making love to the microphone as he spoke into it. Often, I wondered how he was the total package yet, he is not married. I cannot put my finger on what it is, but something got to be wrong with him. Once I saw him look over at me, I blinked away while turning back to my mic trying to save face because I was staring hard.

"For those of you that do not know, this is the session where, yours truly, Heart & Soul, read letters you send in for our advice. You will hear how I feel and how my crazy coworker Heart feel. Let us jump right in it," I stood up and grabbed the letter from the table behind me. The sound of hmm hmmp, slipped from Heart's lips as I walked over to the table. Not saying a word, I sucked my teeth before taking a seat next to him.

As I got ready to speak, I could feel his eyes outlining my body like I was a dead body, and he was the chalk police use. Ain't nothing sexy about that, but he made me feel so delicate under his eyes. The way he stared at me made me feel like he was gently touching me, without touching me.

Glancing over to him, I took him in from the top of his head down to the Jordan's that were on his feet. The fan that I kept close by because I hate being hot had his Jimmy Choo cologne filling the air. I never paid attention to how a guy's bone structure was or if their lips were a perfect match to their face but Coldon was all around sexy as hell.

His full pinkish lips accented his dark skin perfectly. He never wears his hair cut in a low fade, which I told him would look nice on him. Instead, he keeps it low enough so that it curls up with tapered sides. Hearing him clear his throat, I quickly turned back to my microphone while fumbling with the letter.

Dear Heart & Soul

I have been dating my boyfriend for five years now and at first, we would do everything together. Take trips, go to church, family functions and all. We were... in love. Recently he started taking trips without me, not letting me know about his family gatherings until the day of and more than likely, I would have to work that day. He has been catching attitudes with me over crazy things like me leaving the toilet seat down. What type of mess is that? After he argues with himself be-cause I choose not to entertain him, he would grab his keys to leave.

Things went from the honeymoon stage to divorce and he have not even asked me to marry him... YET. Things just feel off, like I do not even know who he is anymore. Valentine's day is coming up and usually he will ask me if I want anything or let me know that he made plans for us, but this year- nothing. I really want things to work be-tween us, but I do not want to be the only one wanting that. Should I stay or go?

Signed, Lonely Girl

"Girrl run!" were the first words that left my lips right when they parted. "What's the song our mommas used to play when we were kids, *"If you don't know me by now, you will never ever ever know me.* That man has pulled a woman move on you. You know how men leave you physically and woman leave you mentally before they physically up and leave you?

He is already gone, passed go and collected those two hundred dollars for gas to get to the new girl's house. The new girl who he is now taking those trips with, sneaking off to her church with because he knows he cannot take her to the church he belongs to with you. Not just that, his family is now making sure she gets that invite instead of you.

Lonely Girl, I would rather be lonely than date a man like that. Five years. Five whole years and you are not engaged or anything. No ma'am, and I cannot stress that "no" enough. You are giving him your good years and he is not giving you anything but his tail to kiss while he leaves you at home and enjoys his life.

Listen baby girl, call him first thing in the morning and tell him to come pick up his feelings, and don't leave no pieces." I quoted Jazmine Sullivan because that's what fit for this situation right here. She needs to tear those feelings up and put them in a trash bag at the door right along with all his shit.

"I'm sure Heart is about to say the opposite of what I just said and that's fine. He is lonely and needs to take a lesson on love from me too. Lonely Girl, get out before you waste any more of your precious years on a man who does not want you."

Coldon Heart

As I stared at this beautiful woman, my stomach turned at the hate she has for men came out of her sexy mouth. Now, I have heard her talk crazy before, but I never thought much about it. I just figured it was all for the show but hearing her now, this shit is boiling on the inside and I cannot help but to wonder what happened.

I have had some messed-up relationships myself, but I never let that turn into me hating all women like she seems to hate all men. The fact that it looks like she is getting off by telling this lady that her man is no good for her, baffles me.

"Heart! Heart!" Hearing Souls, sweet voice call out my name, I snapped out of my thoughts. "What are your thoughts on the letter from Lonely Girl?"

"I don't know about me needing to take a lesson on love from you, but I do know my advice have to be better than what you just said."

"Let's hear it then," she challenged.

"For starters, Lonely Girl disregard everything Soul just said and listen to the Heart speak. Taking big steps towards marriage is huge for men so I get why it has been five years. We overthink and start doubting if we are even good enough to make this woman happy for the rest of her life.

He is probably doing some soul searching and just need time to himself to gather his thoughts. Trips alone, chilling with his family alone, and even church. The only person who feels he is with another woman, is Soul.

The attitude he has is probably coming from lack of sex because I am sure you stopped giving it up once you noticed the change in him. Which is understandable, let me throw that in there. Women just do not jump for sex when you are playing with their heart. I know none of my exes did when I was out there playing games.

Just be patient with him and allow him time to get things in line. Valentine's day is approaching, and you never know what surprises he has up his sleeves. Give us a call or send us another letter after Valentine's day and let us know how things ended up going. Let us know if he was playing games like Soul seems to think or if he was just prepping for a moment that you will not forget. Stay with your man, don't be lonely and bitter like Soul."

We went through two more letters and I could tell that Soul was not feeling it anymore. Her entire attitude went from her being ready to break women's hearts to agreeing with whatever I said. Deciding to end the night early, I turned on a tape so we could talk.

Right when the On Air, light went off, she snatched her headphones off and threw them at me.

"My Soul, what did I do?" Instead of answering, she started swinging on me like she did at the house. Her licks did not faze me, but I still needed to calm her lil ass down.

Standing up, I bear hugged her and started planting kisses on her cheeks repeatedly. I knew she hated when I did that, but it always took her mind off whatever her lil mean ass was angry at me about.

"Is that how you really feel about me?" she scolded while pointing her studded coffin shaped acrylics at me. "You think I'm lonely and bitter?"

"My Soul, I was-"

"Don't my Soul me. That will not get you off the hook this time. Why would you think that?"

"Let's be real Soul, that's the vibe you give off to not just me but to every man with breath in his body. What's the deal with you? It is obvious that you have been hurt. You sit here and use your platform as a prop to pour the hate you have for men into other women. Bashing men like there aren't good men in the world still."

"There aren't." She crossed her arms over her chest then pursed her lips up.

"You know why you keep attracting ain't shit men?"

"Nope, but I'm sure you're about to tell me," she sassed.

"Because you ain't shit, Soul. You are just as bitter as they come. Maybe if you take some time to heal instead of making yourself remember the pain that you felt years ago, you could be happy. Someone good would love to be the man that makes you breakfast in the morning. The man that would rub your feet without you asking him to after you have had a long day.

That great man would pour so much life and love into you that you wouldn't need an app to send you affirmations in the morning." Her mouth opened then shut as if she could not even form a sentence. "Get your shit together Soul. You are a beautiful woman all around. From the curls that beautifully fall over your shoulders. To your cocoa brown radiant skin tone. All the way down to your pretty ass feet, but your soul is as dirty as the subway in New York."

Chapter 2

Soul

I deserve love, compassion, & empathy.

February 1st

T he worst part about hearing everything Heart had to say about me, was that I had to ride home with him. His black Maserati truck smoothly pushed down 285 with, I Want You Around by Snoh Aalegra hissing through his speakers. I softly sung to myself while staring out the window. Trying to ignore the haunting sound of his voice calling me bitter and lonely, in my head.

I began questioning myself as if there were some truths behind what he said. Am I bitter or just tired of men shit? Am I lonely or just like being alone so I will not have to settle for less anymore? Some may see it as that but for me, I'm just protecting my peace. Protecting what Darnell should have instead of breaking me down to a level that now I don't even know if I'm recovering or just covering up the pain that still lies beneath.

"I dated this guy my entire four years of college named Darnell," I finally spoke up to break the tension between us. "When I started college, I promised my parents that I would focus on school and not get wrapped up in things that were going on around campus or with a guy. I was determined to finish school at the top of my class with absolutely no distractions. No parties, no drinking, no smoking, and no sex. That promise I made lasted a week.

One day my roommate and I went to the library to study because they were making entirely too much noise next door. Darnell was there sitting at the only table available with two extra chairs, so we took a seat. It was not long before he noticed that we had the same English Comp homework. That sparked a conversation that lasted until the librarian told us it was time to go.

Everything about our conversation flowed and we did not miss a beat on making it last an extra two more hours once we made it to the steps of my dorm. I must have told him everything it was for him to know about me in less than a twenty-four-hour span.

Even about my little agreement with my parents to swear off all distractions but this one, I felt good about. One night talking all night led to us being in separable. When you saw D, you saw me and that's how it was... for about a month. It was something about him that made me fall in love with him and believe everything he said to me.

He treated me like I was the only woman in the world for him. So, when the girls started doing things to get my attention, I felt like they were lying because that's not the man I knew. The man I knew, was nothing but a big teddy bear. Wish I had known that Barney comes with friendly dick now. That would have saved me three and a half more years of heart break."

"Why stay that long?" Heart interrupted.

"Because not only was he a professional dick-slinger, but he was also a habitual liar. He had me thinking that the girls just wanted what I had and would do anything to take my spot. I was young, naive, and in love. I wanted to believe everything that came out of his mouth so badly that I ignored the truth.

Me thinking that he was the perfect man for me, and then finding out that he was not, made me look at all men differently. It didn't matter how hard they came at me and tried to show me that they were not him. I still could not let the wall that I took so long to build up, come down.

I cried to my mom and she only told me that it is what I deserved because I lied to them about being focused on school," I chuckled, "Can you believe that? My mom blamed me for my own heart break. She did not say baby girl he is just one of a million men in this world and they all will not do you like him. That I will eventually run across a man that was created just for me. Nope, she looked me right in my tear-filled eyes and said, you deserved to have your heart broken."

Just talking about this over again, had my emotions all over the place. I was crying so hard that snot was started to ease out of my nose. Taking a Kleenex out of my purse, I cleaned myself up and tried my best to stop the tears from continuously flowing.

I pulled myself together right when he stopped in front of my condo. He reached and turned the music all the way off, then turned to me. At that moment, I was regretting opening up to him. He hadn't said a word yet, but I don't want anyone trying to sympathize with me and I know this is what he's about to do.

But, when he opened his mouth the words that no one has ever said to me came flowing out, "It's not your fault." He did not say don't worry about it; things will get better for you. He said the words that I've been longing to hear, it is not my fault. I started to believe the words that my mom spoke. Maybe that was my punishment from God because I lied to my parents. If I had never said a single thing to him, things would be ok right now.

Those four simple words made the tears start flowing again. "I hate that your mom said that to you because you didn't deserve anything he had done to you. I'm not saying I'm the best man in the world because I have my flaws too.

I can say all day what type of man I am. How I can provide you with all the finer things in life and that's all true, but I fuck up too. My biggest flaw is that I have everything in the world that would make my woman happy, but I don't know how to love."

When he said that, I sat up in the seat eagerly ready to hear the rest. "My parents were kind of like yours. They wanted me to focus on my goals and dreams. Always strive to be the greatest in whatever I start and whatever I start make sure I exceed all expectations. Money and power were the only things that were instilled in me.

Not to show love, nurture, or to cling to my woman like I was her favorite pair of jeans." I laughed at that part, "I can tell a woman all of the things she wanted to hear that would make her want to give me a chance but when that chance comes, I fall short.

Over the years, I've learned to look at myself as a woman would. Right now, I'm at the point where I am trying to fix me before giving another woman the broken parts of me. I can't afford to hurt the next woman because I don't know how to love her properly.

I don't want her at home begging for me to get off work early because it is our anniversary. Or her asking me to spend some time with her instead of giving her money to shop all day. I may not be a cheater like Darnell was, but I am no better than he is. The only thing that's different is that I've been teaching myself to be the man that you would want one day. I mean that a woman would want one day," he corrected making me side eye him.

"I appreciate your honesty. Admitting to being another ain't shit nigga had to be hard for you," I looked over to him and said.

His brows crashed together before saying, "That's the only thing you took from that?"

"I mean, I just summed up everything you said, that's all." I shrugged my shoulders before reaching for the door handle. Before I could open it, he locked it back making me turn to look at him.

"You're not about to kill me, are you?"

"Really Soul? No, I just wanted you to not say shit like that then run off knowing that's not what it is at all."

"Prove it," I blurted out before realizing what I said.

"What do you mean?"

"You say that you aren't an ain't shit man and that you've been working on becoming a better man, so prove it. Make me fall in love with you. Show me that you can be that guy who showers his woman with love and affection and not just money and dick.

I have a hard time believing the words that come out of a man's mouth and you have a hard time putting actions with the words that come out of yours. Maybe that's what we need, something that would challenge us with what we lack."

Heart

I looked at Soul's mouth move as she said the words, make me fall in love with you. I've known her for three years now and all three of those years, I wanted to do exactly what she just said. Even with her male bashing, I wanted her still and that was because I knew that anger came from a place that had nothing to do with me.

When I first started working for the station, Soul was quiet and more reserved. Over time, we developed a friendship that had us so comfortable with each other that we gave one another keys to our places. You know just for emergencies only.

She would let me in on certain things but her love life, she kept to herself. Shit, she even tried to hook me up with a few women, but I declined. There was no way I could date someone she hooked me up with knowing deep in my soul, I wanted her.

"So, what do you say?" Her angelic voice planted kisses on my ears as she spoke to me. It has always been something about her voice that made a man like me feel a way. I'm too fucking big and stocky to feel a way about a voice but she does that to me.

"I say we take a leave from work for fourteen days, just you and me. No work, no phones unless wear e not around each other, but as soon as we are, the phones are put up. Are you sure this is what you want?" I asked her.

"I'm sure. You really only think it would take you fourteen days to make me fall for you?"

Shrugging my shoulders, I replied, "I don't know but since it's a challenge, I have to push myself to the best of my ability. Shit I'm worried about fucking up. Yea, I've been working on myself but I'm not there all the way yet. "What if I fuck up? Fuck up to the point of you ending up hating me."

"Then you didn't try hard enough," she said while looking out the corners of her eyes.

"What happens if I can make you fall in love with me?" I had to know the answer to this because it is pointless to go that far and there is no reward in the end.

"I guess we will have to cross that bridge once we get there. I'm sure you'll know the next step to take if you can make it happen."

"Just promise you'll go with the flow and won't try to stop me from doing anything. No matter how crazy my plans may get, just let me lead."

"I promise," she replied holding up her pinky finger waiting for me to lock mine with hers. "You are the last hope for all men, if you fuck up, I'm going to studs."

"Forget all of that shit, you just be ready at two, we have a long day ahead of us, my Soul."

"I'll be ready at one thirty, if you are here at two, you are already starting off wrong." I was unsure of how things would turn out between us, but I was ready to see if we both could fix what was broken inside of us. Noticing she still had her pinky up, I locked mine into hers making the most astonishing smile appear.

Getting out, I walked around and opened the door for her. She reached her hand out, and I took it to help her out of the truck.

"You are already starting off on the right foot. You've never opened the door for me before."

"I wasn't trying to get pussy before either. Shit Soul. Your little hits are getting stronger, you better watch that shit." She rolled her eyes at me then started walking towards her building. I watched as her hips swayed from side to side as she walked up the steps.

Normally, I would stay in the car and wait for her to call me to say she was inside of her condo. This time, I followed her up and walked her to the door. Once she unlocked it, she turned around leaning her back against the door frame. She did not say anything, but her face housed a look of uncertainty.

"Let it out," I told her.

"I can't do this, Heart. I don't even know what I was thinking by saying that. We should just do what we have been doing and let whatever happens just happen. We can't force ourselves to fall for each other."

"I don't know about you Soul, but I've been wanting you for a long time."

"Oh," she mumbled with much hesitation in her voice. "I couldn't tell."

"That's because I never tried to make it obvious. Plus, I saw how you clown niggas and I wasn't trying to be that nigga you dogged on the air after he broke your heart."

"See, that's what I mean. You already know that this is not going to end well. I was just caught up in the moment and didn't think about what I was saying."

"My Soul, I was down for all of this and was up for the challenge but if you scared to love me, just say that. I will not put a time frame on it if that would help us out. Just let it flow. Starting by you still being ready by one thirty.

I know you need to go comb your hair so right now you are wasting valuable time on talking yourself out of something that could heal your heart." I could tell she was thinking over what I said so, I started pouting making her laugh. "You pinky promised, Soul," I reminded her.

"Ok, ok, ok! If this date is dumb just know, I'm cutting it short and bringing my ass back home."

"Just be ready," I uttered. She rolled her eyes playfully before pushing her door in and closing it behind her. I smiled to myself while thinking of everything that could go right with us. Let's just pray, I can hold up to my word.

Getting in my truck, it was now five a.m. and I had to go by my brother's crib to check on him. He lives out in Buckhead with his wife Honey. A year ago, he had an accident on his motorcycle that left him paralyzed from the waist down.

Every morning I go over there once I got off to do physical therapy with him. He hated doctors and shit, so he begged me to do it. I knew absolutely nothing about physical therapy, but because my brother only trusted me; I did what I had to do. I started taking classes to at least learn the basics of what I needed to do and focus on, when it came to getting him to walk again.

He has been making a lot of progress and surprisingly he recently started walking. That shit made me proud as hell just knowing I did that shit. Well, me and a whole lot of, *I can't fuck up prayers,* that I sent to the big man above. About twenty minutes later, I pulled into the quiet suburban area he lived in and got out.

Two hours and a bunch of laughs later, I was headed home to get my plans together for Soul. I did not have the slightest idea of what I was going to do but I was going to make the best of the day. As long as, I get to see her beautiful smile at least once, I am good.

Chapter 3

Heart

I have the power to change my life.

Later that day

February 1st.

   Vagary- *an unpredictable or errant action, occurrence, course, or instance.*

T oday it was forty-one degrees and for Soul, that's blizzard weather. She has Lupus so she swears anything below sixty-five is freezing. Instead of doing something outside, I decided to find something for us to do indoors.

She mentioned several times that she loves animals so of course the Aquarium was the first thing that popped in my head. Either that or my homeboy pit bull farm.

Just so she would not be over dressed, I sent her a text before I pulled up to let her know not to put on any heels. Anytime we did anything outside of work, she was always overdressed. She looked good as hell, so I didn't mind then but now she could get as comfortable as she wanted to.

"My Soul, where you at mama?" I asked as she picked up the phone.

"Well since you just now decided to tell me not to put on heels, I have to find something else to put on. Give me an hour and come back."

"Wha-" She started laughing before I could get my words out.

"I'm kidding, come up. I do need about thirty minutes though because you just ruined my entire outfit. Since I have to change clothes, that means I have to do my hair differently to match what I have to change into." Shaking my head, I got out the truck and headed up. She was about to make this more difficult than it should be.

When I walked in, she was walking around in her panties and bra. I didn't know if she wanted me to sit on the couch until she was ready, so since she didn't say, I went into her room.

"My Soul, we can always stay in and you can wear that all day for me."

"Boy don't-"

"I told you about that boy word."

"Heart, don't be silly," she corrected herself. "We are not about to have sex now or any time soon. You can look but don't touch."

"You need to hurry up then because, shit just because." I was at a lost for words as he little frame moved around the room. I'm used to thick women and Soul was everything but that and I still found her so attractive.

"For real though Soul, women should not walk around in front of men half naked like that and not expect them to cross a line. Not on no rape shit or nothing like that but you are fine as hell and that set looks good as fuck on you. Everything about you making my dick hard right now. Just know that the only thing that's on my mind now, is taking that shit off."

"Simmer down playboy. Go sit in the living room and put a bag of peas on your lap. I'll be out shortly. Next time, you'll know to let me know ahead of time where we are going." She started walking back into her closet to pull out more outfits then tossed them on the bed. I still hadn't told her where we were going yet so I took it upon myself to find her something to put on.

Seeing a fitted black jogger suit on her bed, I pulled it from under the stack of clothes. I looked in her drawer and found a long sleeve shit to wear under the jacket. Pulling out her Louis Vuitton boots, since she must wear some sort of heel daily. At least these looked more comfortable than those six-inch heels she glides so gracefully in.

"We are going to the Aquarium Soul, it's really not hard to just find something simple."

"Since you pulled out those boots, now I have to change purses. I can't walk around here looking tacky. Some of us have an image to uphold."

"Soul!"

"Heart, I was joking. I already have what I need in my Montsouris PM Bag."

"You said that like I know the difference in those overpriced ass bags," I added.

Ten minutes later, we were finally on the way. She looked good as fuck and she was not playing about having to redo her hair. It was down when I first came in but now, she pushed it up into this big ass curly puff.

"Don't get none of that juice on my headrest; that shit is hard to come out," I instructed making her eyebrows draw together.

"What juice?"

"That Soul Glo stuff you sprayed on your hair to make it curly like that. I saw Coming to America, I know the lasting effect that stuff has on furniture." She started laughing hard as hell, as if she were about to have an asthma attack.

"Water, sweetheart; just water. A little leave in conditioner but that's it. I'm not those weaved up and gelled down women you are used to dealing with. By the way, what happened to Leslie?" The smile that my face wore was instantly washed away when she mentioned her name.

I looked over at her then turned back to the road without saying anything. This shit happened so fast that I forgot all about Leslie. She and I have been dating a few months now and she is already sick of my shit too. Which is why she pulled that disappearing act on me.

"And you wonder why I can't trust men," Soul mumbled to herself.

"Soul, I haven't heard from Leslie in over a week. The last time we spoke she was pissed about me having to pick you up for work every night when you have a car. When I tried to explain how women should not be out late at night by themselves, she had gotten more pissed off. I told her that women are easy targets, and a lot of shit happens now. She hit me with that, I just think it's funny how, bullshit."

"What did she think was funny?"

"The fact that the night before she said she was hungry. Instead of me going out to get her food, I told her to get whatever she wanted, and I'll leave the door unlocked for her. Honestly, I did not see anything wrong with that because if I had food at the house and you ate that, then wanted more, that's on you. I was not hungry, she was. Plus, I told her to take my gun, that should count for something."

"I would have found it funny as well. You have to think about the things you do and say to a woman. Doing things for me, and then telling her to go out and do for herself, is wrong. She is the one throwing it back whenever you ask, I am sure of it; not me.

Then you get upset when we act insecure if you bring a beautiful woman around. Shit a woman period, then want to act like we have trust issues. No, we have lying, stupid, entitled ass nigga issues," she huffed. "Heart, can you just take me back home please?"

"What? No, I have an entire day planned for us. We are not about to let this conversation ruin the mood."

"Yes, we are. You have so much that you need to handle before starting anything with me. I'm not for drama, exes or current girlfriends popping up on bullshit. I may be small and very pretty, Heart, but I can fight, you know." Her little voice said that with so much power that she almost believed that she would hurt someone.

"I'm not doubting that part at all ma. I just don't see why we would want to throw the entire day away over a conversation about nothing. I'll make sure shit with Leslie is handled but today is still happening for us." I told her bluntly letting her know that I was not changing my mind or turning around. We gone see these damn fish and she is going to enjoy it.

Soul

I don't know what planet this man came from but the men there are obviously imbeciles. Something can't be right in the head of a man who thinks dating one woman and taking another one, correction trying to make another one fall in love with him is ok.

"Who in their right mind would even consider continuing on with a date after a man told her that he and his girl are still together? That not speaking to each other in a while, shit does not mean anything to females.

Especially if she walks up on him and another woman. A woman who she has already shown her insecurities over. That's some foul ass shit and is the main fucking reason I use my fucking platform to call out stupid ass men."

I was beyond heated and this man hadn't found a fuck to give yet because he was still driving towards this damn Aquarium. I would be wrong if I grabbed his stirring wheel and made our asses around. Nooo, but then I'll be called a lunatic.

Pulling out my phone, I scrolled my apps and started acting like his ass was not even in the car right now. After doing what I needed to do, I dropped my phone back in my purse and folded my arms over it.

I kept feeling him glance over at me and each time I would roll my eyes to the sky and turn my lips up. It took him a minute to find a park once we arrived. I got out and stood there pissed because at this point, I wanted to be at home.

Standing back, I watched as he paid six hundred dollars for our entry tickets, parking, plus I tricked his ass into thinking I wanted to do the shark cage dive.

"Here are the wrist bands," he announced as he walked up to me thinking everything was sweet.

"And there's my ride." Turning away, I hustled to Loni's car and jumped in before he could get the words of, *where are you going?* Out of his mouth. "Go girl, go!" I kept looking back to make sure he was not coming to the door. "Why aren't you driving!?" I asked Loni who was just sitting there staring at me.

"You told me your car broke down and you needed a ride."

"Well, kinda," I replied while shrugging my shoulders.

"Well, kinda nothing. You're here with Heart. Why are you running away?"

"Can we talk about this while the car is moving?" I begged.

"Absolutely not, I actually want to go park because I haven't been here in a minute."

"Ok! Ok! Damn. We got off work, had a deep conversation about love and I may or may not have asked him to make me fall in love with him. He was game, but then I asked him about Leslie. He said they have not spoken to each other in a week. I cursed him out, made him spend his money on us to get in here knowing I had already lied to you so you could come get me. There, now drive!" I finished.

"Soul why do you keep doing this to yourself?" She looked at me with sad eyes. When I looked back, Heart was now standing right next to the car.

"What do you mean?" I asked.

"You always sike yourself out of someone loving you. Soul you had no business worrying about the next woman if he was standing there with you. Let him handle that part of his life. Now if she comes to you about him, then you cut him off. But if the man said he haven't heard from the girl then trust him."

Loni has always been the one who does not mind getting me back in line. Even if she knew I would be mad at her for a few days, she still told me the truth.

"What if I fall and he don't catch me?"

"Then that's a risk that you are going to take. Besides, you falling on your little ass might be a good thing, maybe it will grow," Loni teased. "You opened your big ass mouth and told the man to make you fall in love with him and he accepted the challenge. Now you wanna punk out. Nah! Not my friend. You will get out of my car and call me later to tell me all of the details."

"You mean to tell me I gotta go dive with these damn sharks for real?

"That's your fault too. Don't waste that man money, so yes, you have to go take that dive with Jaws."

"Why would you say that?" I dragged as I thought about the movie. "Wonder can he trade those in and see if they got something with Catfish. I would be more than willing to dive and catch a few of them for dinner. Take a few back to Mississippi to my mama and daddy."

"Get out my car friend, and please try to enjoy yourself." Pouting, I got out of the car and stood beside Heart. I'm guessing Loni thought I was going to jump back in, so she drove off as soon as Heart moved off her car.

I was not prepared to answer the questions that Heart was about to spit at me, but I had to. Since I made this bed, I have to lie in it and deal with whatever comes of it. *Lord don't let anything crazy come of it. I'm trying my best to open up even though everything in me is saying bolt and pad lock my heart.*

"For a second there, I thought I did or said something wrong." I looked up into Hearts eyes and gave him a half smile. Not really knowing what to say, I nervously twirled a curl from my high puff around my finger. I tried to find the words that did not seem to care about coming out or not. Clearly, I was looking crazy by just smiling without speaking, like a weirdo.

"You did nothing wrong. I just overreacted and tried to find a reason to not go through with this. Loni was going to be my scapegoat, but she was not having that at all. You see the way she damn near made her car pop a wheelie trying to get away from me." We shared a laugh and that kind of smoothed out the rest of my nervousness. "Heart, can I tell you something about me when it comes to love?"

"Honestly," he paused as if he were pondering over his words. "I would rather you not tell me. Then that would suck the beauty out of making you fall in love with me. I want to learn you, not you tell me what you think I should know. Like the reason you damn near twirl all your curls out of your hair when you get nervous, or the way you fidget with your fingers when you can't find the right words to say.

Knowing you, you will skip the important stuff and have me around here wondering why shit did not work out with us. I want it to work out." He spoke in a tone that gave me the reassurance I needed to throw caution to the wind... again.

Without running, without testing him, without doubting his words, or without holding that pad lock on my heart. Well, I may hold that a little longer, just in case. But he gave me that peace that I needed to pull up my big girl panties and just trust him.

Chapter 4

Soul

I'm worthy of real and genuine love.

February 2nd

Affectionate- readily feeling or showing fondness or tenderness.

I woke up this morning with a feeling of calmness in my spirit. After speaking my daily affirmations to myself, I placed my feet in my UGG slippers then stretched. Getting up, I started lighting my candles in my corner so that I could do a little meditation before I got my day started.

It was extremely hard to clear my head when thoughts of Heart kept clouding my mind. Yesterday was amazing and by the end of the night I pissed that I had to take my ass back home. We started with the Aquarium and I loved it. Once he saw how nervous I was to do the shark dive, he told me that I did not have to do it.

He claims that was the reason he did not do it, but truth be told; he was scared too. We would have been in a cage but large bodies of water scare the hell out of me so I would have drowned from my anxiety.

I'm used to going out and having lunch with him but something about Heart trying to pursue me made it different this time. Him pulling my chair back and holding my hand across the table as he talked to me about something general. The best part of yesterday was Heart listening to me.

That moment I started talking about my mom and he just stared at me the entire time, giving me a stomach full of butterflies. Just thinking about it has them forming all over again.

"When is the last time you heard from her?" Heart asked me after I mentioned today being my mom's birthday.

"I tried calling her before you arrived, but she didn't pick up. Instead of her answering, she sent a text saying she was busy and would call me back later. The conversation was quick and dry. A pure example of short and sweet and I was ok with that. Just getting a reply was good enough for me. At least she sees that I'm trying to patch up the damage that was done."

"By her or you?"

"Shit, her and I guess partially me because I never tried to force a relationship with her. Just like I would a man, I let whatever happens, happen. If we talk, we talk if we don't, we don't. I match energies and act accordingly and that goes for family too." He tilted his head a little and gave me a disapproving look. "What?"

"You can't treat you mother the same way you would treat a man. You can get another man if things go wrong with him, but you can only get one mother. Cherish her because she may not always be around. Fix what's broken before what's broken can't be fixed.

Those words fizzled in my spirit all night long and I was determined to make things right with us. My dad told me they are supposed to have her a party the weekend of valentine's day. At first, I told him that I could not get off when honestly, I did not even try. Now that Heart and I took fourteen days off, I have the time to go and show my face for a little while.

Shoot, I can't even tell you when the last time I drove home. I drive pass that shit all the time while headed to Memphis to see my best friend Jammie. My mom never acts like she wants me to see her, so I see someone who does. No harm, no fucking foul with that shit.

As soon as I took a seat on my pillow to meditate, my phone started going off. I ignored it because now was the time that I set aside for me. I turned on my motivational music and closed my eyes as the music penetrated my soul.

You a paper chaser, you got your block on fire.
Remaining a G until the moment you expire.
You know what it is you make nothin' out of somethin'
You handle your biz and don't be cryin' and sufferin'.

Thirty minutes later, I was blowing out my candles and putting my sage back up. Today was going to be another amazing day. I have no clue what Heart has in store for us today. The only thing I was told was that I could have the day to myself but tonight, I was all his.

If that meant what I thought it did, my morning will be spent getting a fresh wax. My coochie has not been touched by a dick in over six years. I'm not even gone fight him on having his way with me too soon.

It is not like we just met so that should mean a lot. I'ma just lay down and spread my legs. I want him to devour, torture, and pin this pussy to the fucking headboard. At this point, I just want to cum until I am left dehydrated.

Picking my phone up, I saw the missed call from Lori and hit send. "Too late to call back now, I'm already at your door and letting myself in."

"I gave too many people a key to my place," I said to no one in particular because she had already ended the call and walked in."

"You are so ghetto, Soul. Most people listen to soft Jazz or the sound of rain as they meditate. Your crazy ass has Juvenile blasting and expecting that to be soothing." She walked into my room and turned the music down then plopped her thick ass on my bed.

"It's the lyrics that have a lot of meaning behind them, Loni. You're all in my Kool-aid and don't even know the flavor." I joked then stuck my tongue out.

"Red, all niggas like red sis," she retorted making me laugh because she was right.

"Whatever. What are you doing up this early? I'm sure you had a long night with John." She and John have been seeing each other for a year now and she has yet to introduce him to her family. He is the best man she has ever had in her life, but she is so dumb and does not want to take it further.

"Of course, we did but when he told me to get dressed so we could go to dinner I faked sick. He said he's tired of our at home dinners and he wants to take me somewhere really nice."

"Hmp," I let out and sipped my tea.

"Go ahead and say it, heffa. You know you want to."

"You fussed at me yesterday for always siking myself out of being in relationships or just being happy period. Yet, you will not allow him to even show his face. You have him show up at your house with food each time he comes over so he can look like he works for door dash. You don't think he will catch on to that soon?"

"Girl if he hasn't caught on yet, then he won't. I'm just not ready yet. Do you how my family would flip out if I told them I was dating a white man? My dad would shit so man bricks he would be able to build a house. Mama would say dumb shit like, do you want some chicken? They have season on them, and I know that's something your kind is not used to." I was curling over laughing at her ignorant self.

"Mrs. Hill is not that bad. She offers everyone food so he shouldn't take offense to that."

"Did you hear me say the words, *your kind* like he's an alien. She would treat him like he's Mexican and she's Trump ready to build a damn wall in her living room. I can't do it, Soul. Your situation and mine are two different things. Your parents would love Heart. He's sexy, smart, has money, his own place, nice ass cars, tall, beautiful smile, always smells nice, can dress and his dick print looks marvelous."

"Ugh heffa do you love Heart? You know a little too much about his appearance and bank account," I fussed.

"I only know what you tell me and that made me start observing him when he's around you. It was a quick glance and because his dick was on display that day, it only took me a half of second to notice it." Tossing the pillow at her, she caught it and placed it behind her so she could lay back. Loni stared at my ceiling fan for a few minutes before sitting back up. "I'm pregnant, Soul."

As quick as those words left her lips, tears fell even faster. My mouth dropped open in shock as I walked over to sit beside her. Wrapping my arms around her, I placed my head on her shoulder making her rest her head on top of mine.

"I don't know how I let this happen. We have always been so cautious and one time, one freaking time, the condom broke and here I am. Pregnant! Fucking pregnant. I can't be a mom right now; shit I don't even know how to be a girlfriend properly. Soul, what do I supposed to do?"

"Start with breathing." She took a deep breath then exhaled. "Damn, then go brush your teeth. Why in the hell are you outside of the house with your breath smelling like that?"

She laughed before speaking, "Shut up! I had just taken the pregnancy test that John woke me up with and while he was in the shower, I eased out of the house to come here. Once I saw that test was positive, I hauled ass over here."

"You didn't tell him what the test said?" I looked at her like she needed her ass whooped.

"Well, kinda."

"Loni!"

"No, I didn't tell him, I left the test at the door of the bathroom and left. He would have started crying, calling his mama, and then tried to make me call mine. Then I would have to go to Savannah and hear her mouth about having a mixed grandchild."

"You are really overthinking this Loni. It is a baby not a puppy, not a cat, not a new pair of shoes. It is a beautiful baby growing inside of you and you are going to be an amazing mom. Plus, you have me and I'm going to be the best God mother he or she could ask for.

Now stop the crying, looking ugly and dear Lord stop breathing until you go brush your damn teeth." Laughing, she got up and headed to the bathroom. I watched as she opened my cabinet and pulled a brand-new toothbrush from out the pack. I always keep some for when she stays over here.

"Enough about me, what happened yesterday?" Loni stood at the opening of the door while continuing to brush her teeth.

"Everything was perfect, and I hate that I wanted to change my mind at first. He was such a gentleman and made me feel so secure and at ease with everything. Heart has always had this strong personality and made me laugh uncontrollably and he did that plus more yesterday. My stomach hurt all day from laughing at him.

Leslie did not call all day so I'm guessing that was the truth about him not hearing from her. If she were still his girl then she would have called him several times because we were together until like two a.m. Once we finished eating at Slutty Vegan, we came back to my place."

"You guys fucked!" she squealed. "I knew you were going to give that ass up sooner or later. Me personally, I would have given it up the moment they introduced his fine ass as your co-host. Oh shit, John is calling."

"Answer girl, he is your baby daddy now," I joked.

"Can white men be called baby daddy? Is that like a term that's used for just black men?"

"Now that's some racist ass shit. Yes, they ass can be called that as well. Baby father if you want to get cute with it." She finished rising her mouth out then picked up the phone for him.

"Hey baby," she spoke while waving bye to me. Her voice trailed off as she got closer to the elevator. I checked the time to see and noticed I had forty-five minutes to get to my appointment. I showered, washed my hair, threw on something that was easy to slip on and off then headed out the door.

It took me thirty minutes to get to Sweet Samba Sugar and Wax. My girl Tiara always gets me in and out and have this coochie looking pretty again.

Hearing my phone go off, I pulled it out of my purse and smiled when I saw it was Heart. "Hello," I answered trying to sound extra cute.

"Stop it. You know you do not answer the phone like that. Talk to me like you would any other day. I mean when I slide this good dick in ya life, then you can start talking all cute to daddy. Until then curse me out like you normally do."

"Boy what the fuck you want? Is that better?"

"Hell yea, that shit made my dick hard."

"Heart stop, what's up?" I tried to adjust my voice and put the ugly back in it since he said I was trying to sound cute.

"To be honest, I've missed you and I need to see you. It's been almost ten hours since I've seen you and I don't want the image of you to fade away." Pulling my phone away from my ear, I took a picture and sent it to him. "Nah mama, Ima need the real thing. You look good though but bring that ass here," He let out before Face Timing me.

Picking up, I smiled at his sexy ass. "Heart, I told you I'm about to get waxed. I can't go another day with this stubble on my coochie." He laughed as if I said a joke.

"My Soul, how old are you again?"

"Thirty, why?"

"Because that thang is far from a coochie now, it's a pussy and it's supposed to have hair on it. Hair do not stop shit once I open them lips up. It's the clit I'm trying to attack." My heart started beating rapidly because although I wanted to fuck his ass so badly, I never expected him to be so upfront about it. We are both grown and that's what you do but shit now I'm stuck between getting her cute or sitting on this man's face.

"Hush, pussy is too rough for me. Coochie sounds so much better."

"Either way Soul, come here." I started to ask him if Leslie would pop up, but I decided to listen to Loni and just let him handle his own business.

"Soul!" I heard my name being called out.

"What's it gonna be Soul?" Looking between her and the puppy dog face that he was trying to give me. I stood up and walked over towards her.

"I'll have to reschedule; something just came up."

"That's my girl," Heart spoke, making me bite my bottom lip as I stared back into the screen. "Meet me at my house in forty-five minutes. I need to get ready."

"See you soon, my Soul." Ending the call, I jumped in my Benz and pushed it all the way to the house. I got back in the shower and got out just in time for Heart to start knocking on the door. I opened the door wearing nothing but my silk PJ set. The shorts covered all but the bottom of my little ass and the spaghetti strapped tank clung to my body, putting my nipples on full display. He grabbed me up right when he walked into the house without an ounce of hesitation.

"I told you, I missed you," he crooned. "You thought I was lying?" He continued French kissing down my neck like there was icing coating my skin.

I moaned and allowed him to. This nigga had me so hot and bothered, waxed or not I was about to let him fuck my life up. Judging by what was pressed against my abdomen, he was going to do just that. My pussy was leaking, and I most definitely didn't see myself backing out.

His hands firmly held my ass squeezing on it as he mumbled, "You feel how fuckin' hard you got me?" Even as he said it, he lifted me off my feet and sat me right on it. My back hit the wall to the left of the entrance. I was so distracted by the way he was sucking on the tops of my titties that the sound of shit falling from the wall didn't break me out of the haze I was under.

"My Soul, can I make love to you?"

Shhiiidd, if he didn't-

"Shit," I moaned. He pulled my tank down and latched onto my pebbled nipple, groaning as he did so.

"Yeah, I'm about to fuck you good," he stated while carrying me to the living room.

"It's been three fuckin years that I've dreamt about burying myself inside of you," he admitted.

Laying me on the couch, he then removed his shirt. His eyes burned my body from the top of my head to my feet. I watched him grab his dick as he bit his lip, just staring at me. Nervously I bit my lip too. Heart's muscled chest made my mouth water.

"Fuck the couch," he said, scooping me back up. "I'ma spread you out on this bed."

As if I could not do shit for myself, I stood by my bed and allowed him to undress me until I was naked before him. My eyes bucked as he kneeled in front of me. His lips touched my belly button, and his tongue followed, trailing a path to my pussy. Weak in the knees, I collapsed onto the bed. He grunted and pushed me the rest of the way until my back touched the bed.

Spreading my legs wide like he was trying to break my shits. His thick tongue felt like a flame as it stroked my pussy.

"Fuck," I whimpered. Heart's voice is a killer on the mic but the sounds his voice made while sucking and slurping on my box has that shit beat!

I came on his masterful tongue, screaming like a fool. Growling, he quickly stood to his feet and came out of his joggers.

Fuck!

I did not have time to process how damn big Heart's dick was before he was on top of me, with his tongue down my throat and that damn anaconda poking at my middle.

"Let me in, baby." His voice sounded deeper, more sexual than it already was. My mouth stretched as his dick stretched my poor pussy.

"Sooulll...fuck baby," he groaned trying to go deeper. All the while, I laid here in bliss at his sweet invasion. Between how wet I was and the way he gnawed on my lips; I was not sure if I would last long. He put my legs over his shoulders and gripped my hips. He dug his face in my neck as he moved inside of me.

"Oooh," I moaned loud as fuck. My nails tore at the skin of his back as my whole body fluttered. How the fuck did he find my spot that damn fast? Not only that but he was fucking it up! Just like that my body rippled around his thick pole.

"Ughh!" he grunted as I gushed around him. "Soul, you better cum on this dick again, baby!" His words triggered another orgasm, sending my screams into the neighbor's house.

"Heart!" I shouted as he smacked his body against mine, the sound singing sweet music to my already elevated body. He latched onto my nipple, growling, tugging on it as his strokes grew rougher.

"Fuck, I'm cummin' Soul!" he ground out as his fingers dug into my hips. He ruthlessly pumped into me, shouting, "Fuck!" until he was empty.

Chapter 5

Heart

Feb 3RD

I have the strength to overcome any challenges.

Learn- *gain or acquire knowledge of or skill in (something) by study, experience, or being taught.*

I slowly pumped inside of Souls mouth as I anxiously anticipated the feeling of the nut that was brewing. Her beautiful brown eyes looked up at me as her mouth met her right hand in a twisting motion. Slobber built up around her plumped lips, while she took in all of me. I've never seen a woman enjoy gagging, but she seems to love how the tears slid down her cheeks.

My Soul, was sucking my soul out of my body and I loved it. "Fuuuck!" I growled as my cum spilled out the sides of her mouth. Pulling back, she used the back of her hand to wipe the cum from around her mouth. She glared at me right before she licked her hand and swallowed the pretty kids that we would have made if I had cum inside of her.

"Shower?"

"Damn mama, you're not tired yet. We've been at it since I came through the door yesterday."

Smacking her lips, she threw one of her little jabs at me. "I was only asking if you wanted to shower not fuck. As always grab some towels and go into the other bathroom. Or you can go home and come back later and enjoy dinner with me."

"I would rather go home, grab some clothes and then come back over here. That way I will not have to keep going back and forth. If that's cool with you?" Soul got up from the floor and walked towards the bathroom.

"I'll be here waiting once you get back here. Do not take forever or I'll be forced to make love to myself... again. You know like I've done for years. Well, that was until yesterday anyway." Turning back towards me, she walked over and threw her arms around me. "Please don't make me go back to plastic penis and finger puppet?" Confused, I pulled back to see what she was talking about. "My toys," she laughed.

"You have the real thing now; I promise that I'll be right back." I kissed the tip of her nose, then her lips. "Get cleaned up, so I can get you back dirty."

"Hmm yes Zaddy!" Thirstily, she sucked on my lips, then pulled away to head to the shower. Grabbing my things, I headed out the door. My mind was still blown away with how Soul was clinging to me. I wanted to live in those moments forever, but everyone knows that everything that glitters ain't always gold.

These fourteen days might turn out to be the best days of our lives then we can make more memories after. Or these fourteen days could end horribly and would be the worst memories we could have ever made. I'm hoping and praying for the best.

When I pulled up to the house, Leslie's car was parked outside. I knew me coming and leaving right back out was not going to go as smoothly as planned. Taking a deep breath, I stepped out and slowly walked up the steps and inside the house. When I did not see her downstairs, I knew she was up in my room.

"What are you doing?" I asked Leslie who was sitting in the middle of my bed Indian style. Standing up, she walked up to me wearing those tight ass workout leggings that make the females ass look raunchy. Ever since I met her, she has always had crazy sex appeal.

Tall, slim, short hair or a pixie cut is what she calls it. Her skin always looked like it had rays of sun following her around. Even in the winter, her skin would glow. Not today though, today her face carried a look of weary on it.

"Where have you been, Heart? I've been here since last night so before you lie to me, don't." I could not even open my mouth to get a word out before she pushed her finger up to my lips. "DON'T LIE!"

"I wasn't about to lie to you. I was with Soul. She needed-"

"And here comes the lie," she interrupted. "You couldn't just leave it at you were with her without trying to give me some bogus ass excuse as to why you were at her place all fucking night long?"

"I wasn't about to lie to you Leslie. You have been gone for a week. No call, no fucking show. We all know what that means right?" I asked her.

"No, what does that mean Heart?"

"Just like a job when you don't show up your position gets replaced. I was with Soul. She needed to release the orgasms that have been building up in her pussy for six years. Since you said fuck me, I fucked her." The stinging sensation that crept through my face from the smack she just delivered had me wanting to put my hands on her.

"Fuck you, Heart. You are a very fucked up person and I see why nothing ever works with the females you date. You think you can just do what you want to do and never have to deal with the consequences of your actions. Yes, I've been gone a week because I had to wrap my head around what the fuck I had just done.

Now, I'm glad I had the abortion because I would not want my child's father to be as fucked up as you. Bye Heart. I wish you and Soul the best. Lord knows I pray you do not do her how you did me.

I was gone for a week and I did not receive one call from you to see if I were ok, dead, sick, or anything. You did not give a damn about me so forgive me if I do not give a damn about how Karma chooses to come back around for you trifling dog ass.

I pray to the good Lord that you fall so hard for Soul and she hurts you to your core. Someone has to be the reason you change your ways. I tried and it only took a week for me to be replaced. No amount of money, trips or gifts would make me take you back."

"You didn't hear me stop you one time. The only reason I'm still standing here is so that I can lock my door behind you. I need to get Souls pussy juices off my dick then wash my face so I can get her favorite yoni wash scent off my lips."

Her mouth opened and closed before she snatched up her coat then struggled to put it on. I was not for Leslie's shit at all. I did not buy that I am pregnant bullshit because I've never one time fucked her without a condom on. Unless those throat babies were developing; then all of that was all a lie.

When my front door slammed, I locked it and headed straight for the shower. I had already wasted too much time with Leslie and needed to get back to Soul. Her feelings were the only ones that I should be concerned with right now.

Soul

"On a scale of one through ten? How was it?" Loni asked as she and I laid on my floor since she refuses to sit on my bed. Little does she know, we had sex right here too.

"A one," I lied.

"I knew it, all men that look that good always fall short somewhere. Was it his dick? It was small huh? Nah, cause I saw his print, so it was not that. I know, he came before you even got started, didn't he?" I laughed at the things that flew from Loni's mouth.

"I was kidding girl. It was... nice." I paused as flashback played in my mind.

"Nice or nice nasty," she probed.

"Nice nasty. He took his time but still put in work. That man fucked me all types of ways. Ate me from the roota to the toota and back up again. Everything was amazing and I could not get enough of him. At first, I was trying to talk myself out of having sex with him too soon," I admitted.

"You have known each other for years. You have gone to his best friend's funeral with him, have had friendly dinners several times before too. He even has a key to your place, Soul."

"For emergencies only," I quickly added.

"Y'all low key been in a relationship for years just without the title oh and sex. So, trust me when I say, nothing about you having sex is too soon. In fact, yall late as hell on doing it. If it were me, I would have put this pussy on him a long ass time ago."

"You are too much," I laughed. "We are still taking things slow. Today is just day three of us pursuing each other and per him, he gave himself fourteen days."

"And if I were you, I would put this pussy on him for all four-teen. That way, if you don't make it then fourteen days of great sex will last you another six years."

Sitting up, I sat on my legs and looked at her. "You don't think we will make it?"

"I didn't say that Soul, I said if."

"That's the same thing. That means you have doubts of us making it. What if we do and live happily ever after. Would you feel some type of way because what we have may out last what you have with John?" I let out before I had a chance to think over my words.

"Now wait Soul. Let's back up a bit before we say something we might regret. I did not say you would not make it. In fact, I pray you do. You really deserve to be happy and regardless of how many days the love forms, it happened and that is all that matters. John and I are still taking things slow, but I finally planned a dinner for our parents to meet and to tell them about the baby.

We are not about to jump into marriage although he did ask me once I made it back from your place yesterday. I just pray this dinner goes well because my mom's opinion means a lot to me."

"You shouldn't let your mom control who you love Loni. No matter the color or sex. Love is-"

"Something your lil mean ass didn't know about just three days ago," she teased.

"I knew what love was, and I knew what I expected it to feel like as well. I just have not trusted anyone to give my heart to them after you know, Darnell. Love existed but only for others, me, not so much. I want to be loved beyond the moon and the stars. I want to be loved by someone who only wants my heart to beat at the same rhythm as theirs. Someone who knows all my flaws but still see me as flawless.

I love the random pictures taking of me while we are out at dinner while I am staring at the menu. Or for me to sit on the floor surrounded by work, completely exhausted and he walks in and tell me how beautiful I look. Why can't I have that?"

"You can and you will. Just do not run from it when you feel it coming. I know you and the first sign of you falling for Heart, you will do something to push him away. Open your heart up Soul and let him show you his. If he fucks up, at least you know you tried." I smiled at her making her frown up at me. "What?"

"How do you have all the advice in the world but you letting ya mama have a say so in who you date? Last time I checked, ma didn't even have a man and she may or may not know who your father is."

"See, nah! You be doing too much. I told you that in confidence."

"And I just told you the truth to your face. You just don't want to hear the truth."

"Neither do you," she retorted.

"Wait, we are doing all of this back and forth and you rushed over the part of you saying John asked you to marry him. What did you say?"

She held up her hand and showed an empty finger. "I told him no. I wanted to say yes but then it just didn't feel right. With us not meeting each other families and I'm even scared to date him outside of the house."

"Loni, is it your mom or is it you that just haven't gotten over the fear of being judged by the outside world? If you have not noticed, everybody and they daddy have interracial relationships. They do not care anything about what nobody thinks. I think you are using her as an excuse, and you need to stop," I told her honestly. When the tears started rolling, I knew I hit a spot that she was not ready to speak on yet.

"Soul, look at me? I do not look like you and I've been judged all my life. I've finally gotten to a place where I am happy with myself and the way I look and now here is another battle that I have to get through. My black ass dating a white man."

"Are you serious? You are beautiful Loni."

"Yea, for a dark skin girl, right?" I was taking aback by the words that left her mouth. She has never told me anything like this before. Since I have met her, it always seemed like she was confident in herself. She can pull any man that she wants, she got a natural banging ass body and her real hair damn near touch her ass.

"I've never once looked at you like that. When I say you are beautiful that's the end of that compliment. No buts, you are beautiful boo and as soon as you feel that, you would stop caring about what someone else thinks. So what John is white, but name one Black man that you have dated that has treated you better than him. And honestly you can take race out of the conversation. Even if he were black, he has still treated you like his queen.

There is nothing that he would not do for you and as far as I've seen, there is nothing you would not do for him either. Be happy friend because just like I deserve happiness, you do too." Leaning in, we embraced each other and let out a few tears.

"Lord this is going to be a long pregnancy. I've been crying since I found out."

"Don't forget to add the fact that you are a cancer. We are some emotional ass people, period. Now let us get up because I've spent too much time with you and should be getting ready for Heart to come back over." Getting up we walked out of the bedroom and stopped in our tracks. "Heart, what are you doing here?"

"I've been sitting in the living room listening to y'all cry for thirty minutes now. The conversation seemed important, and I didn't want to stop you in the middle."

"How much did you hear?" Loni asked?

"I heard enough to add to everything that My Soul said. You deserve to be happy, and color should not even be a factor. If John makes you happy then that's the only thing that matters. Same as you Soul."

My eyebrows raised and my ears opened as soon he said my name. "We've known each other for three years now and there's nothing that we don't know about each other. These fourteen days are not for me to fall in love with you because I've been there.

These fourteen days are to reassure you that I'm better than the man I used to be. I know you love me, even if you are not in love with me. It is still love there and that's all I need to get everything else in line for us. Now kick your girl out because all of these tears and love talk is making my dick hard."

Seeing Loni eyes slowly go down to his print, I nudged her in the arm. "Ouch," she shouted before walking to the door. "Treat my girl right Heart. Oh, and make sure things are over with your and Leslie cause pregnant or not, we will jump her."

"Stop Loni, we will not jump that girl," I turned to Heart and told him.

"Cool you don't have to join in, but just know I'ma tag her." Laughing, she walked out the door.

"I didn't hear you come in." I beamed as Heart wrapped his arms around my waist, pulling me close to him.

"That is the beauty of having a key. You can sneak in and eavesdrop on deep conversations. I learned a lot about you and her. She's lucky to have a friend like you and I'm lucky to have you as well."

He kissed me on my forehead then walked me to the bedroom. Undressing me, he then did the same before climbing behind me in bed. We did not have sex we just laid there and talked. That was the first time I had been naked, and nothing happened. The form of intimacy he gave me was far beyond what an orgasm would have felt like. Just being body to body with him gave me all the pleasures I needed.

Chapter 6

Soul

February 4th

I am the master of mt energy

ENERGY *the strength and vitality required for sustained physical or mental activity.*

Waking up the next morning, I handled my hygiene before doing my morning routine. Heart was still stretched out across the bed with my thick covers wrapped around him. I turned my motivational music on low before lighting my sage and candles. Sitting down on my pillows, I closed my eyes and started saying my daily affirmations.

Feeling my pillow sink in, I opened one eye only to see a naked Heart sitting next to me. Closing my eye back, I mumbled, "I know you don't have your ass sitting on my pillow?" Instead of replying, he laughed.

"I'm sorry but this looked interesting, and I wanted to join in. Plus, this used to be one of my favorite songs so when I heard it playing, I woke up to see where the party was at."

"Shhh," I hissed. "Go put your boxers on then come sit back down. Please and thank you." Kissing my cheek, he got up and went to the bathroom. I heard the water running so I figured he jumped in the shower. His phone started going off back-to-back. Getting off the floor to put it on silent but the lock screen caught my attention. I took a seat on the bed and scrolled the messages from Leslie.

Les: *You really doing this right now?*

Les: *I've been through too much to help you build yourself up to be a better man and you let that trick reap the benefits of it.*

Les: *Nall, I'm not even going to let that happen. I'll fight for you no matter how long it takes.*

Les: *I lied about getting rid of our baby. I was away for a week trying to wrap my head around being pregnant.*

Les: *We have a baby on the way Heart, aren't you happy?*

Les: *You have five minutes to reply to me before I come knock on her door and drag you out of there.*

After reading that text, I jumped up and started putting my sweats on because she must be crazy if she thought about knocking on my door. Before I could get out my bedroom, Heart was coming out of the bathroom.

"What's wrong mama?" Heart gently grabbed me by my arm to turn me towards him.

"Leslie, that's what's wrong with me. She is texting you like crazy. Not only is she saying she is still pregnant by you, but she said she's about to knock on my door if you don't come out in five minutes."

"Nah, I'm not letting you get into anything with her. It is my job to handle anything pertaining to her and not let any drama or harm come to you, your home or anywhere around you.

I will handle her, and you finish meditating. I promise, I got you and she is not going to bother neither one of us again. Now go be a paper chaser and clear your head." He joked about the song that I was listening to.

Heart dried off and threw on some sweats and a t-shirt. A loud banging started on my door causing me to jump up.

"Nope, I told you I got you. Go sit down."

"No, I'm not about to let her disrespect my house like she has lost her gah damn mind."

"My Soul, let me handle this, please," he begged.

"No, I see how you handle things already and apparently this is the outcome," I shouted back.

"I SAID LET ME HANDLE IT. NOW GO SIT CHO LIL ASS DOWN SOUL, NOW!" Doing as he said, I went into my bedroom and slammed the door. Pulling my toy out of my nightstand, I laid across the bed and started playing with myself. It was something about the way his ass just put me in my place that made me horny as hell. I know I could have waited until he came back inside but I'ma still be mad at him by then, so it is best I get this out the way now.

Heart

"Leslie, I told you this between us was over. You were never pregnant by me because I always wrapped my man's up. You can say it is mine all you want to, but I know if you are pregnant, it is by another man. A whole week Leslie, a week you were gone, and you want me to honestly believe that it is because you found out you were pregnant. Which is a dumb ass lie.

You know everything about me so that means you know I would be a good as daddy and if you were pregnant that you would not have a damn thing to worry about. Being pregnant is nothing that you would have waited a week to tell me. So, stop with the lies and let this shit go.

I'm good where I am so don't contact me, don't contact nobody in my family, don't show up at my job, and yo ass better not come over here no more. If you see Soul out, you better not even think about parting your lips to her, or we gone have a bigger issue than you faking like you're pregnant by me."

"But Heart, I love you," Leslie cried out.

"But I don't love you." Turning away, I headed back inside and locked the door behind me. When I walked into the room, Soul was in the shower. I started to wait in her room on her to get out so we could talk but I decided to go cook her some breakfast instead.

Knowing her favorite was French toast, cheese grits, eggs, and bacon; I made all of it with orange juice for her to drink.

"Is this your way of saying that you're sorry for bringing drama to my door after I told you I do not do drama or exes?"

"No, this is my way of making you breakfast because it's early as hell and I know you are hungry because I am. I do owe you an apology for Leslie popping up over here."

"And the baby?"

"Isn't mine and I doubt if she is even pregnant. The baby is not something we should worry about at all."

"Is Leslie someone that we should worry about," Soul asked as she took a bite of her French toast.

"No, she knows not to bother either one of us again. I told you she has not contacted me in a week. When I went home yesterday, she was already there and asking where was I at all night. I was honest and told her that I was with you. That is when she started the, she was gone for a week because she had an abortion.

Then for her to pop up today saying she is pregnant; that she did not have the abortion is crazy. I do not have time for that at all. My focus is you. Once she saw I was not feeding into the mess she was trying to cause, she left. Then today it was this. She has some issues and I'm not about to be a part of nothing she has going on."

"That was the first and last time I'll allow something like that to happen. I am trying my best to go with the flow with you Heart, but I promise you I do not mind stopping. No matter how good you make breakfast," she stuffed more eggs in her mouth and closed as eyes like they melted on her tongue or something. I thought it was cute.

"I promise, I got you my Soul."

Chapter 7

Soul

February 5th

My body is my temple, take care of it and it will take care of me.

NURTURE- *the process of caring for and encouraging the growth or development of someone or something.*

My body was aching all over when I woke up and I could hardly move. Usually when I get like this, I just lay here until the pain goes away because I hate taking my medication. This time, the pain was unbearable, and I had to call someone over.

Heart went to his brothers early this morning, so I did not want to bother him. Picking up my phone, I called Loni to see if she could swing by.

"Hey boo!" she answered with enthusiasm.

"Hey," I replied in a groggy tone.

"Aww pooh, what's wrong?"

"Aching like crazy. You know I hate taking those strong ass meds and I'm all out of ibuprofen."

"John and I are headed to my mom's, but I can stop by the store on our way out and bring you some."

"Thank you so much. Let yourself in, I'll be in bed." Ending the call, I laid across the bed and I tried to force myself to go back to sleep. I found out I had Lupus in twenty thirteen. When I first got the call from my Doctor's nurse, and she said that I have Lupus and Rheumatoid Arthritis, I cried so hard.

I had never heard anything positive about people having lupus, so my first thoughts were, I am going to die. She did her best to calm me and let me know that they are all types of medication that they did not have years ago. She told me if I stayed up to date on my medicine and stay compliant with my doctor, that I will be fine.

So far, what she said was true, I am just hardheaded and do not follow instructions well. Eleven pills a day is nothing that I want to do for the rest of my life so I go without as long as I can. That is until the pain gets like this, then I take something.

"Soul! Soul!" I opened my eyes as I felt my body being rocked back and forth and my name being called; it was Heart.

"Hey," I smiled through the pain.

"I got your medicines for you."

"How did you know I needed medicine?" I inquired.

"Loni messaged me on Facebook and told me that she thought she would have time to go by the store for your medicine and asked if I could. If you were not feeling well baby, you could have just called me. I would have come to you sooner." The way his voice sounded so concerned and caring made me smile even harder.

"Why have I pushed you away all of these years?"

"Because I wasn't worthy of your time then. I was not ready for a woman like you then, but I am now. Like steak, love needs to marinate so it can be the best you've ever had." Winking at me, he helped me to my feet but when he saw I was too weak to stand, he sat me back down.

"I don't want you to ever wait this long before you take your medicine again. You are doing more harm than good to your body Soul." Nodding my head, he lifts me off the bed and carried me into the bathroom. Sitting me on the toilet, he started running me a bath. I watched as Heart moved around my bathroom and bedroom getting the things I needed.

"Does soaking in a warm bath help?"

"It does." He went under the cabinet and pulled out my muscle relaxing Epsom Salt. Once he checked the water to make sure it was not too hot for me, I instantly fell in love with him. That simple gesture broke down my walls and exposed my heart and soul.

"It's ready." Standing up, he undressed me then helped me get inside of the bubble bath. "I'll let you soak for a little while, then come in to bathe you. If you need me before then, I will be right in the bedroom. Just call my name Soul, and I will be here.

The water felt so good as my body relaxed into it. I must have soaked for thirty minutes before Heart peaked into the bathroom to check on me.

"You ok, my Soul?" Heart's voice was so soothing.

"Yes love, I'm fine. You can come in." He came in and took a seat on the side of the tub before grabbing my towel and lathering it up. Gently, he washed my body, making sure he cleaned every part of me.

"Soul..."

"Yes, Heart?"

"I love you." Hesitation had me stalling to reply. I knew what I wanted to say because I have always had love for Heart, but it is more than a friendly type of love now. When he kiss me, my body gets this tingling feeling. Butterflies form in my stomach and my nipples get hard. The moment he wraps his arms around me, I melt. And the way my pussy clings to his dick like saran wrap made me see that I was made for him. Why else would he fit so perfectly inside of me?

"I love you too." He released a breath after I said that as if he was holding it in.

"You sure? Is it like you love me like you love you sister or brother?"

"I don't have either one of them so I can't answer that. I love you like a woman loves her man. Nothing friendly about it. I have always had love for you but the simple act of you testing the water for me made me fall overboard. Or, made me see that what I thought was a friendly sign of love, was for sure the real thing. I really do love you Heart and I'm ready to see where this will go."

"It's going to go as far as we make it go. I promise to always be honest with you and to put you first. I want to be with you every second of the day and planted inside of you every night where I will eventually lay my seeds. It took me three years to get you my Soul and I promise that I'm not letting you go." Tears weld up in my eyes, and before they fell, Heart kissed them away.

Lifting me out of the tub, he took my purple towel and wrapped it around it. Laying me back on the bed, he started drying me off with the towel. Slowly, he would dry off a spot, then kiss it. His lips felt so good and made my body start craving him. I could feel the heat and moisture forming between my legs.

Moans escaped my lips as he kissed up my inner thigh. A single kiss on my pussy lips then a double on my clit. Heart wrapped his big arms around my thighs, holding me in a position that locked me in place. Even if I wanted to run from his tongue, I could not.

"Hmm," I moaned when his wet tongue folded my clit up then released it. Only for him to continue over and over but now in a gentle sucking motion. My thighs trembled, my eyes rolled, and my voice whimpered out a cry of ecstasy.

"You taste so good," Heart hummed into my pussy like he

was playing the harmonica. The vibrations sent my body into overdrive causing me to climax instantly. Dipping his tongue inside of my pussy, he then slowly dragged his tongue down to my asshole. Aggressively, he squeezed my ass cheeks, pulling them apart so that he had a full view.

The sound of him spitting on my pussy, turned me on even more, without warning, he came up a slammed into me. He did not care about me getting adjusted to his size.

"If you want to rip me in half, just say that" I joked.

"I'm sorry mama, I had to feel you; all of you." Pressing his body to mine, he nibbled on my ear while he continuously pumped inside me with vengeance. Both of my legs were lifelessly hanging over the creases of his arms. With every stroke, I watched his stomach muscles tighten and release.

"Fuck!" I moaned out when his dick hit my g-stop. Once he heard that, he knew he was in the right place and he was not letting up.

"Cum for daddy," he growled. His breathing picked up and he was now sounding breathless. Flipping me over on my stomach, he laid on top of me and slid back inside of me. I loved this position because I was able to really grip his dick as I matched his powerful thrust. "Fourteen days my Soul. In fourteen days, I don't want you to be in love with me, I want you to be my wife," he let out making my eyes buck. Biting my bottom lip, I pushed back, forcing us into the doggy style position.

"Don't just say that because my pussy is good," I told Heart. Throwing it back forcefully, he stopped me and held my hips in place. Neither one of us were moving but I could still feel his dick pulsating inside of me.

"I'm saying that because that's what I want. Fuck the time, fuck the order of operation and all that shit. I have you and I do not want to lose you, Soul. Marry me!" I didn't' reply because I was not about to accept a marriage proposal like that. If this was really something, he wanted then he needs to ask me properly, not during sex.

Slowly, he started sliding back and forth inside of me. "Fuck Heart!"

"Don't run."

"I can't help it, shit," I moaned out.

"Take your dick Soul." Pulling out, he laid on his back and tapped my thigh, gesturing for me to get on top of him. On top is where I stayed as I rode us both into powerful orgasms.

Chapter 8

Heart

February 9th

I look fear in the face, and wink

Need *require (something) because it is essential or very import-ant.*

For four days, we have been cooped in Soul's condo and today we finally decided to come up for air. I loved being under her but the last thing I wanted her to do was get tired of me. I have never been the clingy type but with Soul, it is an instant magnet, and I can't break loose.

Although she has not complained one bit and seems to enjoy the way she has been spoiled, I decided to still give her a break today. She made another appointment to get a wax with Loni since she had to cancel the first one.

I told her I didn't care about hair but if I had known she grew hair like a chia pet, then I would have waited those thirty minutes or so the first time she was there.

Glancing over at her, the sun was shining through an opening in the curtains and beaming on her face. She looked so beautiful while she was sleeping. Moving her curls out of her face, I kissed her cheeks softly before rolling out of bed.

I needed to jump in the shower so I could get this day started early. I needed to go holla at my brother about Soul. Since I promised him that I was coming over to talk and not work, he has been holding me to that all week long. Which was cool because I love chilling with him.

He is walking better than he was, so today I was getting him out of the house. This would be his first time leaving since his accident and I am sure there is a lot his ass wants to do.

Getting out the shower, I dried off and walked out the bathroom with the towel wrapped around my waist. Soul was still sleeping peacefully, so I decided to get her morning routine started for her. Lighting the candles and sage, I fixed her pillows that she usually sits on and turned on her favorite motivational song by Juvenile.

As if the music was her alarm clock, she sat up in bed and smiled. "What are you doing?"

"I have to get to my brothers, so I started your routine for you so that's one less thing you had to do. Just in case you wanted to jump in the shower, this step is already done." Walking over, I did my usual, kissing of the forehead and cheeks. "I'll be back but if you need me before then-."

"Call you!" she finished. "I love you and be safe."

"I love the way those words roll off your tongue."

"Come let something else roll off my tongue," she was practically begging for the D that I did not have time to deliver.

"Tonight, I promise so be ready. Go handle your business and don't forget your pussy maintenance appointment is at nine-thirty."

"I won't forget, trust me. It looks like I have on a synthetic wig down there." Laughing at her crazy ass, I grabbed my keys and headed out the door.

∞ ∞ ∞

Parking in my brother's driveway, I got out and headed inside. Honey was in the kitchen cooking breakfast while he was at the table staring at her. My brother Pure was the man before his accident. Women used to fall at his feet, but he only had eyes for Honey. Since they met in Elementary School, it seemed like every class, they had it with each other.

Shit even college, they were truly a match made in heaven. The difference between Pure and I, was he ignored our family views on love and followed his own path. He was able to get money and bring his woman with him.

Showing her that even with other women coming at him, he was still all about her. Pure has never cheated, never called Honey out of her name shit they hardly argue. How can someone have a perfect relationship is beyond me, but I am here to learn as much as I can from him now. Usually, I would run from the conversations about relationships because I thought I knew it all; I didn't.

"Hey Cold," Honey spoke. She always joked about how our mother named us Colden and Purity Heart. It was weird to me too. It was as if she knew one would know about love and one would be cold hearted. I do not allow anyone to call me Cold and Honey knows that that's why she is smiling at me now. "I'm sorry, Heart."

"Yea whatever, you know better than that," I playfully scolded.

"Nah she doesn't because nobody puts her in her place but me. If she calls you Cold, then that's what it is. Besides, that's just your name and it doesn't define who you are." Agreeing with him, I took a set at the table right as Honey placed a plate in front of Pure and I.

"I'll let you two talk, I'm going up stairs." Honey kissed Pure on the forehead and walked out of the kitchen.

"What's wrong?" He asked right when she was out of our view.

"Why you ask that?"

"Normally you would come over, do this lil therapy shit and dip. So, when you told me you were coming to chill and get me out the house, I knew something was on your mind; or someone."

"It's Soul," I admitted.

"The pretty ass girl that works with you?"

"Yea... her. She and I are trying to see where we can take things between us. Well, she told me to make her fall in love with me. We have been together every day since February 1st, and everything has been good. She told me that she loved me, and it wasn't in a friendly way."

"You have been working together for a minute now. I am surprised that you have not tried before. The chemistry between you two is crazy. I can see that shit and you know my vision ain't the best," he joked, and he wasn't lying either. Pure ass needed glasses since he was in pre-k, damn. "What's up with Leslie?"

"She and I are done."

"Just make sure you aren't moving on too soon. I knew nothing would come of you and Leslie. She was not your type. Soul is more of the type of woman I have always saw you with. You need to be with someone who is headstrong. Someone who will not allow you to just get by with the little things you can do to please them.

She will require more time, more patience, and more love. Be gentle with her heart and if you truly want things to work with you, be honest about everything. Anything dealing with your past, your parents, shit even me if it is stopping you from being a good man to her.

Honey and I have been together for almost our entire lives. I will never allow another woman to hurt her feelings with something that I did with them. The sex is amazing so why would I ever go looking for it with someone else. Honey has all I need plus more.

Soul has that for you to, you just have to bring it out of her. It's there but she just has her guard up because she knows how you are with women. Show her that Coldon, heart isn't cold like his mama made him out to be," we laughed.

"How dare you guys talk about me like I don't stay here too." Mama walked in the kitchen and kissed us both on the forehead.

"Technically, you live in our guest house," Pure told her.

"And you are wearing out your welcome there," Honey came in and added. "Morning ma."

"Don't morning mama me, after you just told me to go home." Mama took a seat next to me and pulled my plate of unfinished breakfast in front of her. "Since she didn't make enough for me, I guess I'm left to eat these scraps."

"You weren't going to eat that because I wasn't done. You just took my plate without asking," I snapped.

"Don't sass me Cold Heart."

"It's Colden ma, stop doing that. You are the reason I'm sitting here now at thirty years old trying to get love advice from my brother."

"Tuh, he's been with the same woman for years, what advice does he have to give you? You have to be with more than five people to know what love really is. One woman can't challenge your mind and your heart nearly as much as five different attitudes can."

"Which is why you are in our guest house instead of at home with your husband?" Pure spat back at her. "You will not keep coming into my home and disrespecting me or my wife. You needed a place to stay, and we opened our home to you. This isn't just my place and if you want to stay here until daddy say you can bring your mean ass back home, then you need to check attitude."

"I don't have to take this. I raised you two and you will not disrespect me."

"Ma, you came into our house with an attitude. How do you expect us to react to that? You can either fix that unnecessary attitude or leave. Simple as that." Pure stood up from the table and walked up stairs.

"Fix you attitude or leave," mama mocked him. "Who does he think he is?"

"He's your son and he's a grown man who deserves to be respected in his own home. I agree with my husband one hundred percent. Either respect us and our home or go to a hotel." Honey gave me a hug before walking towards the stairs. "Heart come back another day, I'm sure Pure isn't up to doing anything now since your mother just pissed him off."

"Tell him I'll call him later on." Nodding her head, she then headed up the stairs. "Why do you always start shit with them?" I turned to my mama and asked. "They were nice enough to let you stay here for a few days and so far, it's been a month. I would have been tired of you too by now. Go home mama and fix things with daddy. You aren't doing anything but ruining their relationship because you don't like her."

"No one said I don't like her, she's just not good enough for him."

"In the eyes of who, you? The way you feel about her does not matter. Pure loves her and that's what it is." Shaking my head, I pushed back from the table and grabbed my keys. I couldn't take no more of her negative bullshit.

Soul

"How did the dinner go?" I asked Loni as we looked over our menus.

"Surprisingly, it went well. Mama liked him more than I thought she would and was not surprised that he was white. I think my sister big mouth ass had already told her just so she wouldn't act shocked once they arrived."

"His mom and dad are so nice and loving. His mom must have hugged me and rubbed my stomach every time she walked past me. I thought it was cute and very soothing to see them take to me like that. They said they were tired of seeing pictures of me and not my beautiful face in person."

"See, you were worried for nothing," I told her.

"Now when are you going to see your family?"

"I supposed to leave out in the morning."

"Is Heart going?"

"I didn't ask him to but I'm sure if I did then he would. I will only be gone for a few days and I am sure I will not need backup during that little time. They are having her a party and if she has any type of sense, she would be on her best behavior." At least I pray that things will go smoothly. Mama can show her ass at times, especially with me.

"If you need me to come with you then let me know and I'll come stay the night with you and we can leave in the morning."

"I'll be fine boo, thank you." We sat there a little while longer before the waiter came over and took our order. I loved how Loni has always been willing to drop everything and be by my side. She is the true definition of a friend. I have never once doubted her words or that she would ever say something about me to anyone else in a bad way. Nothing I have told her has ever been repeated back to me by someone else. Everyone should have a friend like her.

"Where's Heart?"

"He's supposed to be at his brother's house for a little while today. We have been so attached to each other and decided to take some time to ourselves. I would hate for him to get tired of me already."

"Girl, Heart loves you and I don't even know why you've never saw it. When I told him you were sick, he replied instantly about leaving his brother house right then to get to you. Even before you did this little challenge thing, the love was there. With that powerful ass dick, he is slanging if you don't be in love in fourteen days, you shonuff will be pregnant," we both laughed.

"I will not get pregnant. Neither one of us are ready for kids just yet."

"Good, because Heart already got a baby on the way." Loni's head dipped around and so did mine when we heard a voice from the booth behind us. Leslie slid out of the seat and stood next to our table. I could not even get my words out fast enough before Loni stopped me.

"We will not address bullshit. If she is pregnant then time will tell and so will Heart. Until then we will finish eating and let this trick go on about her business."

"Smart move." Leslie blurted out.

"Just know that I am pregnant too and if Soul can't beat your ass then I surely can. Stop playing in my friend face." Leslie smirked and headed out the door with her lil friend.

"That girl is really trying me. Do you know she had the nerve to pop up at my house the other day? Banging like she's the police and shit."

"Why didn't you tell me that before I let her walk away?"

"Girl, sit down, she is not even worth it. Let us finish eating and go shopping or something. That belly will be growing soon, and you'll need some bigger granny panties." Loni started pretending to choke on her drink.

"First the fuck of all, I would walk around with no panties on before I wear anything over a size seven. Seems like the bigger the ass, the higher the price to cover it. Ain't nobody got time for that. Plus, with this new pretty kitty I just got, I need John to be able to have full access. Panties would be in the way."

"Shut up! Hurry up and eat, I'm missing Heart."

Chapter 9

Soul

February 10TH

I am safe and secure.

AMEND to change or modify (something) for the better.

I had just gotten off the phone with Heart when the snow had started to come down and freeze once it hit the ground. I was halfway to Mississippi before I hit some black ice coming off the bridge and started spinning out of control. Luckily, my dad had a friend that lived close by and he was able to help me out.

Heart begged for me to allow him to be with me, but I told him that I was ok. When I slid into the median, my front tire got stuck so they towed my car to my dad's friend shop.

It took my daddy about an hour to make it to me and I was so happy to see him. I am a daddy's girl for sure and with me being the only child, I have always been spoiled by him. When I wanted to get away from them, it was mostly my mom who was the problem.

"Thank God you made it back home safely. You had me worried Soul." The way my mother rushed over to me had me scared. She was nice, a little too nice and my daddy laughed once he saw the look of terror covering my face as she hugged me.

"Be cool," he whispered while walking past us.

"Um hey ma, how are you?"

"I'm fine now that my daughter arrived here safely. I was so worried about you on that highway by yourself."

"I'm fine mama, don't fret." Moving her hands off my face, I stepped back to remove my coat and scarf.   I could not believe my crazy ass decided to come here a few days early to spend time with them before her part on Friday. I could have just waited until then, less time to deal with this fake love she is showing me now.

"What's up with her?" I asked my daddy who was tucked away in his man cave. Shrugging his shoulders, he took a puff of his cigar and exhaled the smoke. "She's high, just wait till she calm down. She will be her old self again.

My mouth dropped open before I yelled out, "She's high? What do you mean, she's high?"

"One of your cousin Alley friends, sent her some edibles from New York. It has been helping her with her pain or knocking her out one. Either way, I like her like that. I crumbled a brownie up in her coffee before I left to get you. I knew it would kick in right on time."

Shaking my head, I took a seat next to him on the cough. "I've missed you."

"Then why is this your first time coming home?"

"To be honest, I come by here all the time to see Jammie. I would let mom know and she would just say ok, have fun and get off the phone. It seemed like she liked me being away, so that's where I stayed... away."

"You have more than one parent. Even if she did not want to see you, you still could have stopped by to see me. Do not ever stay away this long without coming to see me again. Life is too short for you and your mother to keep acting like kids." Placing one hand on my shoulder, he pulled me over to him and hugged me. "Things will get better between the two of you. Time heals all wounds."

"Daddy, I don't even know why she still holds this grudge against me. Yes, I started dating in college, but it's not like I got pregnant and dropped out of school. I still finished on time and did what I was supposed to do. She has never once said that she was proud of me. You've expressed it a lot but her, never."

"Don't worry about her, I'll keep her high long enough for you to enjoy yourself while you are here." Hearing the bell ring, I got up to answer it. When I looked through the window and saw who it was, I ran to the door and swung it open.

"Jammie! What are you doing here?" I squealed while embracing my best friend.

"Your mom called me and told me you were on your way here. She was extra happy, and I had to witness this moment more than I had to see you. Something wasn't right with her at all."

"Same thing I said, daddy said she's high." I whispered.

"Ah shid, where my gul at? Let her know I got that good shit in my purse." Jammie is straight Memphis through and through. The opposite of me which is why I call her my alter ego.

"I hope you didn't bring that stuff with you."

"Soul you know I never leave home without it. I needed it to function." Shaking my head, I helped her with her bags so she could get settled into the guest room. Mama was walking around the house singing Betty Wright.

After the pain, we sit, and we talk awhile. And I fight with all might to hold back these tears from falling with a pleasant smile.

Jammie pulled turned away from me and danced over to my mama who was now in the living room. She joined in with her as me and my daddy watched them give us a show. Both seeming like they had been hurt before.

And after the rain, I can't believe you got the nerve to still call me baby. And I try to tell you, "No, it ain't so," but I guess "No" just ain't in me.

∞∞∞

"How's everything going?" Heart asked me. I was on Face-Time talking to him while everyone else was in the kitchen eating.

"It's going ok, I miss you a lot. I wish I would have told you to just come. We could have gotten a room and laid up until Friday. Now I have to lay up with my bestie."

"Don't act like you don't love me, bitch." Jammie plopped down on the bed next to me and snatched the phone out of my hand. "Damn friend, he fine." She looked at me and then back at him. "Hey, my best friend boyfriend."

"Hey Jammie."

"Don't be polite with me. I am hood as fuck. Before I give this phone back to my friend, I want you to know that I am very over-protective of her. If you hurt her, I'll send them Crips at you."

"Jammie!" I let out while laughing. Don't tell him that."

"You already know me, Soul. Now back to you Heart. She already told me about your ex. Let her know that she has no more times to pop up on my friend or I'm coming to Georgia and shut-ting it down."

"No need for that because Soul already know that I got her and I'm not letting nothing happen to her. But thanks for the warning." Jammie passed me the phone back then left out the room. "Mama Katie, smoke one." She yelled as she walked down the hallway.

"I'm sorry baby."

"No need to apologize, it's good to have friends like that. Es-pecially with you being so timid."

"You ain't thought. I told you before not to let the cute face fool you."

"Keep talking tough, you gone make me pop up and steal you away for a little while. I've gotten so used to sleeping next to you that a nap didn't even feel right without you."

"Aww baby, I'll be back on the thirteenth. So, make sure you have something dope planned for our last day together." The look on his face was one for the books. I could not do anything but laugh.

"You're not in love with me Soul?"

"I was just playing, Heart. Don't be so sensitive."

"You didn't answer my question. How do you feel about me, my Soul?" I was quiet for a second while I thought over my words.

"Heart, I know I haven't been this happy in years. You make me smile uncontrollably just by you walking into the room. It seems like ever since that stuff happened with my ex and I, that I have been holding my breath. Now that we are in this moment with each other, it seems like I can breathe again. I want to thank you for giving me my breath back.

Thank you for opening my heart. You said you did not know how to show love, but you have been doing that for me since we started working together but I just could not see it. I had wool over my eyes, and I could not see the man that was in front of me. From the cute gifts you would give me for Christmas and birthdays, that I would only look at as a friendly gesture.

The nights I would miss work because I was under the weather, you would drop off soup on your way to work. And I would do the same for you. There were layers of you unraveling before my eyes. We have been making sacrifices for each other long before these fourteen days were even thought of.

These past three years we have been building a foundation for what we are standing on now. I love you Heart and I'm ready to be yours and spend the rest of my life with you." I wiped the tears from my eyes that were falling. He stared at me with a face that matched mine. I have never seen him shed a tear besides at his best friend funeral.

"Soul this whole time I thought I didn't know how to love but the truth is I just was trying to love the wrong person. This with you came naturally. We did not have got force the feelings or the attractions we have had for one another. I told you the other day that on that fourteenth day I would ask you to marry me, and I meant that shit. I'm about to pack a bag right now and we about to turn your mom's birthday party into a family gathering."

"Wait, what are you talking about Heart?"

"I'm about to get my mama, daddy, Pure and Honey. We will get a hotel, but I need to meet your family now because I am about to steal their daughter away from them. I love you Soul. Text me the address and I'll be there by Friday morning."

Without allowing me to say anything, he ended our Face-Time. I was so in shocked that I did not know how to react to what he just said.

"What's wrong baby girl?" My dad asked as he rested on the door.

"I think I'm about to be engaged."

"What do you mean you think? Either he asked you or he didn't? And who is this guy, anyway baby girl? I didn't know you were dating."

"Daddy, it's a long story and according to him, he and his family will be here for mama's birthday party to meet you guys."

"Good because no one is marrying my baby girl without my permission." Knowing he was serious, I hoped things went without a hitch and I pray mama have enough edibles to last all weekend.

∞ ∞ ∞

Feb 12th

I deserve everything

"Today was the day of my mom's party. My baby and his family arrived here safely this morning and I was so happy to see him. He even surprised me by bringing Loni along with them.

Mama has been on her best behavior and seems to be getting along quiet well with Mrs. Heart. Mr. Heart and daddy been in his man cave since he arrived, so I take it things are going smoothly between them as well. I was happy this moment finally came and now I am patiently waiting on what was to come of all of it.

"Where we gone do it at?" I heard from behind me.

"Huh, what are you talking about?"

"I thought you called me in the house to have a quickie?" Heart stated while turning me around to him and planting kissing all over my face and neck. I have missed this so much.

"You know I didn't say that, but we can sneak off to my tree house. It's big enough."

"You have an actual tree house?"

"Ugh yea, who didn't?"

"Me."

"Well, I was a spoiled little girl so when I asked for a tree house, my daddy and uncles came through. Now do you want this quickie or not?"

"Not, because it's time for the party to start and we do not have time for these shenanigans." Loni and Jammie stood in the hallway, blocking us from coming down.

"Girl if you don't move. I have not seen my baby in a few days; I need this." I told Loni while trying to push them out of the way. They both were bigger than my little fragile ass and was not moving no matter how hard I pushed. "Forget it. Shoot, I don't even want it anymore." Pouting, I folded my arms and looked between the two of them.

"You can go to the kitchen and help us cut up this fruit," Jammie insisted.

"Fine." They moved to the side to let us go by. When they did, Heart and I bolted past them and headed out the door, straight to my tree house.

Heart

After finishing our quickie in the tree house, Soul and I went back inside of the house to clean up. People started to arrive, and sex was the last thing we wanted to smell like.

Once I finished, I headed right to her dad's man cave so I could have a talk with him. I prayed he gave me his blessing because I would hate to disrespect this man in his house and ask her anyway.

"What's up youngin" her father spoke as I walked in and took a seat. He poured me a glass of Jack Daniels then passed it to me. "I was wondering when you were going to come talk to me. You've been avoiding me since you arrived."

"I wasn't avoiding you. It's just been a few days since I saw Soul and I wanted to spend some time with her."

"Understood. What's on your mind?" He was asking questions as if he already knew what I wanted to ask him.

"I wanted to ask you for your permission to ask Soul to marry me. We've known each other for a while now and-"

"I'on give a fuck bout none of that shit, bout none of that shit. I'm kidding, my niece had me watching tiktoc with her earlier and we made a video to that one." I had to laugh because that shit through me off.

"For real son, I don't even care about all of that. My answer is yes. Soul would not have allowed you into my home if she did not love you or thought for one second that you were not the right man for her.

She has been hurt before and that caused her to pour cement over her heart. If you were good enough to chip through that cement without breaking her heart, then you are all right in my book. Welcome to the family son."

∞∞∞

Everyone was in their own zones and having a good time. I looked over at Mr. Heart and he nodded at me to go to the DJ booth. Taking a deep breath, I got up and walked over to it. Asking for the mic, he turned the music down making everyone fuss, including her mama. She was either drunk or high, becasue she was the loudest person in the house asking what happened to the damn music.

"I'm sorry, I know you are enjoying the moment but right now I want to turn this moment into something bigger. Can my beautiful woman come up here please?" Soul slowly approached me with this look that scream, *OH MY GOD, OH MY GOD, THIS IS IT,* without her even saying the words. I wanted to laugh but I had to keep it together.

"Are you sure you want to do this right here?" Soul mumbled. Ignoring her, I pulled her closer to me.

"My Soul, when I first met you, I thought you were the prettiest woman I had ever seen. Working next to you every night caused me to love everything about you. The way you dance when our food would arrive. The cute snort that you would let out when I made you laugh."

"And I hate it," she laughed and snorted, making everyone laugh.

"But it's so adorable to me. When you challenged me to make you fall in love with me, I thought for sure I was going to mess this up. I managed to mend your heart that was broken for six years. Like you told me early, that everything we have done for each other since we met was only building a foundation for this moment.

Now that I have my Soul, I never want to let you go. I promise to always love and protect you. To wake up before you and start your morning routine for you so it is one less thing you have to do. I promise to make you laugh more than I make you cry unless it's tears of joy."

Bending down on one knee, I whistled making everyone including Soul, look at me funny. That was until she saw this little toy poodle running towards me with a purple bow around her neck. Picking her up, I untied the ring that my brother placed around her neck. Soul took her out of my arms then kissed her.

"Heart she's so cute," she squealed. Soul looked down at me when she felt her hand being lowed to me.

"Soul Tyes, will you marry me?"

She was so excited that she dropped the dog causing her to run off. Soul looked at the ring with wide as and screamed, "Yaaasss!!! YES HEART! I'll marry you." Everyone cheered as we embraced each other. As the tears slipped from my Souls eyes, I kissed them away so that she would not ruin her make up.

"I love you, My Heart."

"I love you, My Soul."

Epilogue

Soul

The Heart wants, what the Soul desires.

February 14th

I woke up to a bed of roses, and gift bags all around the bed. We arrived back in Atlanta late last night and it looks like Heart already made plans for today. Getting up, I scrambled through the bags pulling out everything inside.

There were gifts from the new Jimmy Choo, I want Choo perfume, the Chloe Marcie medium leather satchel that I have been eyeing for weeks now to a new pair of red bottoms. There were six more bags that I had not had a chance to open before the bedroom door came open.

"Heart, I love everything baby," I squealed as I ran up to him and wrapped my legs around his waist.

"I knew you would, now get down baby. You need to put some clothes on because we have a chef here for the entire day ready to prepare your favorite breakfast, lunch, and dinner. After breakfast, I have a set up for a couples massage. They should be here around eleven.

"You did all of this for me?"

"From here on out baby everything I do is all for you. Today is just a taste of how the rest of our lives will be. I know I told you that I did not know how to show love without buying things. Now that I have learned to tell, that does not mean I have to neglect showing you as well. Just promise me that you will trust me and know that I'll always have your best interest at heart."

"I promise, baby."

$$\infty \infty \infty$$

Feb 15th

Heart

"It's time for our Heart and Soul love letter session. We have been out for a minute, so I am sure our emails are full of letters for advice. Soul's heart has been fixed with Gorilla Glue so I am sure she will have better advice then what she was giving before.

I would also like you to know that Soul is officially off limits. I'on want you chumps sending no more emails up here asking her out on a date or I'm tracing them then coming over to holla at cha, you feel me?" Soul turned off our mics and started laughing.

"You are really crazy."

"Only about you."

"You guys forgive my crazy fiancé. He is nowhere near as mean as he sounds. In fact, he is a big teddy bear." She leaned over and gave me a kiss on the lips. "I love your crazy man."

"I love you more, mama."

"Let us jump back into this session and see how everyone's valentine's day went. I want to add that mine was perfect, my man got me everything I wanted and some things that I did not need too. The best gift was him asking me to marry him and of course, I said yes! And oh my gawd the ring is gorgeous."

Winking at me, she started tapping on her laptop and pulled up a letter. "I found two letters for us to start with, one

I'll read and it's one that's addressed directly to Heart." Confused about the letter, I clicked the email she just sent me then smiled at her once I read it.

Dear Heart and Soul.

It is me again, Lonely girl only this time I am not so lonely. Just as Heart stated, my boyfriend asked me to marry him. He was not cheating or doing any of those things that Soul told me. He was simply clearing his head and preparing to ask me the most important question ever. I said yes with no hesitation and I cannot wait to invite you to our wedding. Thank you for giving great advice and the invitation will be in the mail.

Not so lonely girl!

"For the first time, Heart's advice was right. Usually, it is my advice and these men do turn out to be nothing but dogs. I am glad this one turned out in your favor. You deserve to be happy boo and I wish you nothing but the best. Now, I'm going to turn the mic over to my lovely fiancé so he can read his letter before our commercial break."

"When Soul sent me this letter to read, it made a tough man like me smile from the inside. It is a simple letter, but you have no idea how much power these little words hold. This one is address to me and it reads."

Dear Heart, I trust you!

Love, Your Soul

The End

Made in the USA
Columbia, SC
01 September 2021

44704988R00052